The
Hook-Up 4:
The Finale

HD CAMPBELL

CHAPTER 1

"Hello," Yvette answered, after accepting the charges from St. Louis County Jail.

"What's up Vette?" Spitter asked.

"Shit. I really need to know what we got up to get revenge on that bitch Keysha and her punk ass friend Harvey."

"Hey girl, hold that down," Spitter cautioned. "They might be bugging our shit. I don't trust nobody."

"Look, I don't need you acting like a bitch right now! That bitch Keysha and her boyfriend had my baby daddy killed. I'm not just gonna let that shit slide!"

"What you wanna do?"

"Robb had a lawyer who got him off. He kinda shady but knows how to work the system. I'm gonna hook you up with him. His name is Jim Starkey."

"Okay. You think he can get the charges dropped?"

"I think so, but I'm sure he can do more than that public defender of yours who's only paid to babysit your case like he's in a damn daycare or something."

"Aiight, bet. When can he start my case?"

"I'll have him hit you up in the morning."

"Bet," he replied.

CHAPTER 2

The next morning Keysha leaves the doctor's office with her son in a stroller when she runs into Harvey wheeling in his girlfriend Stephanie who has also come for a visit. It was an awkward meeting. Harvey and Keysha hadn't seen each other since the night of the incident.

"Hey," Keysha awkwardly greeted.

"Hey," he awkwardly responded.

"What's going on?"

"Nothing, just taking Stephanie in for therapy..."

"And therapy is waiting while you're trying to catch up!" Stephanie angrily snapped at the both of them.

"Well, I'd better go," said Harvey. "You take care of yourself."

The two parted ways as Harvey walked into the doctor's office. With the appointment scheduled, the two were already set to see the therapist.

Keysha walked out confused by Stephanie's attitude. She understood about Stephanie being in a wheelchair but didn't understand the bitterness. Could it be Stephanie had time to fester about her condition, the condition Keysha had off-handly caused? Or did she blame Harvey for his part in bringing it all on. Either way, Keysha was curious as to what was going on.

Knowing she still had Harvey's number, she sent him a quick text: *Harvey, I know I'm the last person you want to hear from right now, but this is Keysha. Is everything okay with you and Stephanie? Let her know that I'm sorry for my role in her being in the chair. If I can do anything, please let me know.*

She put her phone away before getting in her car and driving off.

CHAPTER 3

"Stephanie, I'll be honest with you," the therapist started. "With the injuries you've suffered, you shouldn't be alive. Thank goodness you are, and let me be the one to tell you that the road is long but we expect a full recovery."

Harvey replied, "That's wonderful..."

Stephanie snapped, "Will you hold on! You interrupted the doctor."

Harvey tried to ignore the way Stephanie talks to him, but he finds it hard daily. Just then, his phone beeps. He takes it out as he continues to speak. He discovers it was a message from Keysha. He read it but deemed it inappropriate to reply to right then, though he had to admit it that made him smile.

"Harvey, are you listening to the doctor?" she snapped again.

"No baby, what did he say?"

"If you were paying attention instead of being on your phone, then you'd be able to hear what he said for yourself."

"Sorry baby but…"

"Are you arguing with me?" she snapped.

"Ahem," the doctor interrupted. "If we can continue, the spine isn't completely severed and can heal effectively over time."

"That's great!" Harvey replied.

"Great for whom?" Stephanie asked. "You're not the one in this chair. Your ex whore or whomever got me in this and..."

Harvey stood up and turned to walk out.

"Where are you going?"

"Right now, we're in a doctor's office. I don't have time to fight or argue with you. This is not the time or place for this conversation. I'm here to see you get well because I love you, but all you've done is beat me up. I don't need your blood pressure heating up any more than what it is.

So call me when your session is over, and I'll pick you up. In the meantime, I have some thinking to do."

CHAPTER 4

Harvey walked out and went to the car. Before starting it up, he looked at the message on his phone. Instead of answering the text, he called her back.

Immediately, she answered. "I never expected you to call me, much less call me right back. Is everything okay?"

He didn't know how to answer. Despite his history with Keysha, he felt comfortable talking to her. He also believed that if it wasn't for the whole Susan fiasco, they would have be together even as we speak.

"Not really," he volunteered. "I'm not sure what's going on with Stephanie."

"Have you seen things her way?" Keysha asked. "She's in a wheelchair over some shit we put her through. You have to think about that."

"You're right, but I'm doing everything I can to help her."

"That's just it. You're doing *everything*. Maybe you should dial it back just to see how much she truly appreciates you. Do you guys live together?"

"We talked about it, but no. I'm going to have to move because she can't do the stairs. I can't move in with her because her apartment is too small for both me and my son."

"Sounds like you guys are in a dilemma."

"No, the living space isn't an issue. In fact, it makes it easier to get away from her at times."

That statement gave Keysha an involuntary orgasm.

"Harvey, are you back to your old ways and cheating again?"

"Nope, but the sex hasn't been there either. I don't blame her, so I've just been chillin'."

The conversation rang a lot of the right bells in Keysha.

"So what are you doing now?"

"Nothing. I'm chillin' until her

therapy session is over."

"Well, do you want to chill over here? I promise we'll just talk."

"I don't know," Harvey hesitated.

"I promise; we'll be good."

CHAPTER 5

That was the conversation, that's how it was supposed to be. However, between the end of the talk and the time he arrived at her house, it had both of them craving so much more. The second Keysha opened the door wearing a very short blue and red striped dress with no shoes and what looked like no panties, Harvey's dick jumped right to attention. He realized he'd missed her just as much as she missed him.

The two immediately embraced each other and started kissing the second he entered. Harvey's instincts kicked in as he pushed her to the bed and started eating her cookie.

"Aww damn, Harvey! This isn't what I meant by talking, but damn keep talking!"

He sucked her clit and stuck his tongue as far as he could inside her. She squirmed and squirmed until she let out a powerful scream in ecstasy. He then started grabbing her breasts and tweaking her nipples still eating his meal between her legs.

"Damn Harvey! Harvey! Harvey!" She repeatedly called his name out in pleasure until his face was drenched with her love juice, a flow which he gulped down proudly.

Keysha then told him to move back while she took off her dress and then started taking his clothes off. She then immediately sucked his dick, sending Harvey into another world. Harvey just couldn't resist the feeling of pleasure.

"You've grown since the last time I saw you. You need to give me some right now!"

He pushed her onto the bed and then grabbed her big legs putting them over his shoulders before pushing himself inside hard and deep.

"Damn boy! You have gotten bigger. Scared of you."

Rising her big ass by her legs, Harvey went in deeper...deeper...and deeper until she exploded again. Then he went for his, straight fucking her until they both exploded yet again.

He then collapsed beside her. Both recovered like prize fighters after a match.

"Damn boy! Do you even realize we're the same mess we got into the first time?"

"Yeah, but this time, I need to know what this is?"

"This is two adults getting our rocks off because neither of us is getting the love we deserve."

"Got that right."

Harvey continued talking about how Stephanie started being cold to him after the incident.

"I can understand her being upset with me, but it's been months and it

THE HOOK-UP 4: THE FINALE

hasn't cooled yet. I'm trying to do what you say and see things her way but..."

"Harvey, I was just talking shit because I know you care for her. You owned up to your shit, and you're still there. Sometimes I believe you're a bit naïve."

"Why do you say that?"

"Don't get me wrong. I believe most nice guys like yourself are naïve. You stuck with me and didn't challenge me about the baby. After I tried to pin a baby on someone and it turns out not to be his, most men wouldn't let me live that down. You, on the other hand, let that shit go, and you're here. After we broke up the first time, you took me back and even helped me after Robb's shit."

"Well, I was forbidden to see you after the shooting incident."

"Harvey I understand. I know I was a bitch. I was a bitch to you and your girlfriend because I was still trying to get all I could get from you. Again, most men would see that and treat me like shit about it. However, you still wanted to fuck with me."

Harvey sighed and said, "not naïve really. I'm just a nice guy, and nice guys have to go through the most shit because of who we are."

"What do you mean?"

"If I was just a typical nigga just out for some pussy, I'd get a lot of passes. I wouldn't have to jump through as many hoops. Us nice guys, we can't be nice because you're always looking over your shoulder wondering what my game is. We're not about games; we're just looking for someone to love and to love us. That's not too much to ask."

"No, it's not."

The two embraced for the longest time naked on the bed before engaging in a kiss. The kiss sent them back into a passionate state. This time they made love in a loving embrace. The passion could be felt between the two all over the bed.

"Oh Harvey, I missed you so much."

"I missed you too."

They kissed.....

They touched....

They fucked.....

They filled more than each other's love parts. They filled each other's hearts.

"Damn Harvey, where did you get all of this passionate energy from?"

"I don't know, just missing a Keysha in my life!"

Moaning as she spoke, Keysha replied, "damn boy! I need to take a hiatus from you more often.

Outside, Yvette had driven by Keysha's house and parked when she saw Harvey's car.

"Ohhhh yeah, this is even better," Yvette said. "Y'all have y'all little fun now because when Spitter get out of jail, it's on."

CHAPTER 6

Back inside, the two were on round three when Harvey's phone rang.

Getting his voice together, he answered, "hello."

Stephanie on the other end replied, "uhhhh! Can you pick me up?"

"I thought you had another hour."

"Well obviously I don't if I'm calling. They weren't going to overdo it on the first day. Now come and get me; it's cold out here!"

Harvey hung up.

"I'm tired of this shit, and I'm going to tell her too."

"Can I call you tonight?" Keysha asked.

"You better call me tonight. I'll be home."

Harvey quickly got dressed and then washed his hands of the Keysha smell before leaving. He kissed her one more time before leaving. When he got in his car, he didn't notice Yvette watching him as he drove off.

CHAPTER 7

It took about twenty minutes for him to return because of the traffic, but for Stephanie, it was twenty minutes too late.

"Nice of you to show up!" Stephanie said loud enough for people to hear.

Harvey remained silent until he got her in the car. They drove off.

Being nice, he asked, "shall I take you home?"

"Did I ask you to take me home? Don't you even care what the doctor said? Damn you're stupid!"

Pissed, he immediately pulled off the road into a parking lot so fast that he scared Stephanie.

"Are you fucking crazy? If you're going to be like this, I want to go home."

Harvey immediately went off.

"You know what, Stephanie? I am going to take your ass home! Then I'm going to arrange transportation to and from your appointments because apparently I'm pissing you off by just breathing!"

"What the hell are you whining about now? I just said..."

"You know what? Forget it. I'm

taking you home."

Without a word, he drove off and took Stephanie back home. He immediately took a shower and fantasized about his earlier encounter with Keysha. He then chilled until it was time to go pick up his son.

CHAPTER 8

The next morning in court, Spitter was released on bail as Yvette had predicted.　He was out by that afternoon.　The second he walked out of the jail, the first figure he saw was a car, and on it sat a caramel colored woman with short shorts, pink sandals, and a top that almost exposed her nipples.

"So what's up?" Spitter asked when he entered the car.

"Revenge on that bitch, Keysha. But first, I know you ain't had a good fucking in a while, and I know you niggas inside ain't bonding like that."

"Damn! You fine and all, but you my boy's gal."

"Your *boy* is six feet under right now. And for being loyal, I know you'd take care of me in case he was either locked down or gunned down. I ain't had no good fucking in a minute, and I know you haven't. So you better come take this pussy while it's wet, nigga."

"Right here?"

"Yeah nigga, you scared?"

"Naw bitch. So give me that pussy then!"

"I love a man who's forceful."

The two fucked in the car right outside the jail, ignoring any caution coming their way. They fucked hard for about twenty minutes until they both got their problems resolved sexually. Then the two got dressed.

"Now that you know you can get it whenever you want, I need you to focus on the task."

"Oh, that's cool. I need to kill that bitch Keysha for getting my boy killed."

"You need to kill Keysha, Harvey, and possibly that bitch Stephanie."

"What's up with that nigga, Boo? He fucked up big time. He even fell in love with that bitch, fucking up the entire plan."

"Don't worry; we have a surprise for him. Anyway, he's not even fucking with her. Keysha stopped talking to his ass not too long after the funeral. In fact, he's our first target."

CHAPTER 9

That same afternoon, Harvey was in the gym when his cell phone rang.

Getting off the treadmill, he answered.

"Hello Stephanie."

"Harvey, please don't hang up. We need to talk."

"About what?"

"I think we do need to part ways."

That statement threw a curveball

into Harvey's soul. While he was relieved to not have to deal with her attitude, another side of him was hurt that she felt that way.

"I'm sorry about my attitude, but I don't want to keep taking this situation out on you. I need to get this therapy done and take some time out for me."

"Okay then."

Before she said another word, Harvey hung up the phone on her. He walked out to his car and drove over to Keysha's to only find she wasn't home.

He sent her a call that went straight to voicemail.

"Great!" he yelled. "What the hell else could go wrong?"

He then drove away. He was headed home when the phone rang. It was Keysha.

"Hello."

"Harvey, Boo's been killed in a drive by!"

"Wasn't that your boyfriend? The one Robb hired to…"

"Yes. They said Spitter is out of jail, and he did it. I'm scared."

"Where are you?" Harvey asked concerned.

"I'm at the police station. They called me since I was his emergency contact. Can you please come get me?"

"Yes. I'm on my way."

Harvey turned around and went to

the police station to meet Keysha.

CHAPTER 10

While Harvey was headed to the police station, Spitter who was also sitting in front of Keysha's apartment, called Yvette.

"'Sup," Yvette said, answering the phone.

"You'll hear about Boo in the papers. It's done."

"Damn nigga! You quick and dangerous. That's a fucking turn on, nigga. You need to come back here

36

and tear this pussy up!"

CHAPTER 11

About thirty minutes later, Harvey arrived at the police station to pick up Keysha who was a nervous wreck. She was silent on the trip to the car. Harvey truly understands the hurt that she feels. He's been there before with the loss of a loved one.

He was driving towards her house when she said, "Harvey, this isn't a come-on, but I really need to stay at your house for a few days, if you don't mind."

"No, I don't mind."

"I'm not putting you or your son out, am I?"

"No. Let's go get your son; we can all stay at my place. I'll even order pizza and Netflix. It'll be on..."

His words were interrupted by Keysha crying.

"Did I say something wrong?"

"No! In fact, you said all the right things. It's just me. I've fucked you over so many times. You've done nothing but be nice to me. But this time, I'm doing right by you, and I still get fucked over. I broke up with Boo but was considering giving him another chance. I was going to give you and Stephanie a chance to..."

"Stephanie broke up with me

earlier today. The attitude she had with me was just her way to drive me away, and it worked."

"Oh damn, Harvey! I...I don't know what to say."

"It's for the best, Keysha. I've been developing real feelings for you. The only problem is they didn't fester until we bumped into each other yesterday."

"Damn, I was just thinking about getting back with Boo and this happens. What is the universe trying to tell us, Harvey?"

"I don't know, but I wish it would hurry up and get done with us."

"Amen to that."

Harvey drove Keysha to pick up her son and then his son before going back to his house.

CHAPTER 12

Over the next few days, Harvey and Keysha ended up growing closer than ever. They talked more, they made love more, they grew a friendship. It was something they'd never established.

Three nights later, they went to a restaurant inside the Moonrise Hotel. Harvey was dressed in a black suit with a blue tie. Keysha was dressed in a nice blue flower dress and black shawl. Her pumps were peep toe blue. The two had a nice romantic evening that led to a night of pleasure within the hotel.

Little did they know that they were being spied on by Yvette and Spitter who were in the next room. The two listened to them have sex, and it got them hot as well. While lovemaking was going on in one room, fucking was going on in the other. However, when Yvette and Spitter were done, the two smoked blunts and talked.

"So what do you wanna do about the bitches in the next room?"

"Nothing right now. We'll let them have their fun. Besides, I have another idea."

CHAPTER 13

The next morning, Harvey gets up to go the restroom and make some of the hotel room coffee. Hearing him get up, Keysha turns on the television to discover breaking news.

"Harvey!" she screamed. "You may wanna come in here!"

Harvey ran into the room toward the television. Apparently, his ex-girlfriend Stephanie was killed in what looked like a home break-in gone wrong.

That sent Harvey into a very bad state. His body sank to the point where he immediately had to throw up. Afterwards, the two held each other and wept. Within a month, they both had lost a lover, but Harvey was seeing more than just a coincidence.

"Wait a minute. How in the hell do you lose a lover and I lose one within a month's time?"

"I don't know Harvey...I don't know."

"No, baby, think about it. All of this happens just after Robb gets killed. What the hell? What about Spitter? Is he out?"

"Spitter?" Keysha laughed. "That fool don't have the good sense God gave him, and even if he did, he would still need to read the instruction manual. Even if he was out, he wouldn't be the one setting these things up."

"Not without help, of course," Harvey added.

"Yeah, but who would help that fool?"

"Someone else. Who might have problem with Robb getting shot by the cops?"

"I don't know, Harvey."

"I need to go to the police and get some information. I'm going to let them know what's going on or what I think is going on."

"Why get them involved at all, Harvey? I don't really like cops."

"You asked me a few days ago why

the universe is out to get us. I can finally answer that question. The universe is out to get us because we haven't been right. I met you under false pretenses. I started this bullshit. It rolled downhill from there. I want to be with you, but first, I need to clean up the mess I started.

CHAPTER 14

Harvey kissed her and went to the police station.

"Excuse me," he said to the desk sergeant. "I'm here to see the lead officers on the Stephanie Brown case. I'm her boyfriend."

Harvey was taken to the homicide department where he met Detective Gene Weinstein.

When he approached Harvey, Weinstein led him to an interrogation room.

He asked Harvey to have a seat and then he said, "for starters, you're not under arrest and you're not a suspect. However, we do know you're involved indirectly."

"So do you know who did it?"

"That depends. Do you know who Dontavious Jackson is?"

"No."

"Maybe you know him by his street name. Spitter."

That name sent shockwaves over Harvey's system. "Yes, but we're not friends."

"Oh trust me; we know you're not friends. His only friend was shot by police a few weeks ago."

"Are you talking about Robb?"

"Yes. I believe he's getting revenge, so we need to get you and your child some protection."

"Protection? I thought he was in jail."

"Not any more. He was bailed out days ago. That's when the murders began."

"Murders?"

"An ex-boyfriend of your friend Keysha was killed."

"Oh, Boo! Yes, she's staying at my house now."

"We know. We've been following you since..."

Detective Weinstein's phone started ringing.

"Weinstein."

He held the phone while Harvey watched his facial expression contort during the call.

"Okay...Harvey, we have to go. There's a situation at your house. We may need you. Possible gunshots!"

"What?!" Harvey asked.

CHAPTER 15

Harvey followed the detective to his car. During the trip, several thoughts went through his head.

What about his son?

What about Keysha's son?

What about Keysha?

When Detective Weinstein said gunshots, he thought about Spitter and how he may have killed Boo and possibly Stephanie.

During the drive, Weinstein said, "one thing just doesn't fit Harvey. Spitter is a yes man. I mean, he's tough and a gangster, but he's no criminal mastermind. In fact, he's more of a henchman, for lack of a better term. I just don't know who could be pulling the strings for him."

CHAPTER 16

At Harvey's house, Spitter had the two kids held at gunpoint while Yvette had Keysha naked in a chair slapping her around.

"Bitch, you had my man killed! Now I take that shit rather personally."

Keysha yelled, "no! That nigga had himself killed for hitting me and fucking with me!"

Yvette punched her with a closed

fist. "Naww bitch! You shouldn't have fucked with him in the first place. This bullshit you and Harvey started, I'm going to finish it tonight, and you don't know how I'm going to do it. Hell, I don't know how I'm going to do it, but you're going to die *tonight!*"

Tears rolled down Keysha's face.

"Oh you scared? You scared? You weren't scared when you fucked my man and played him. You weren't scared when your snitchin' ass called the cops because you can't take your licks like a fuckin' woman! You weren't scared when the police shot and killed his ass. Maybe Spitter need to come in and have his way with you. He's the only one who didn't have his way with your hoe ass."

Yes, Keysha was scared, but not for herself. In even this state, she thought of her son and Harvey's son. It was then she realized she loved Harvey more than she knew. She didn't care about herself; she wanted Harvey and the kids to be safe. She then reminisced on how she first met Harvey. She met him under false pretenses but later started developing feelings for him.

"What you thinkin' about, bitch?" Yvette asked. "You wondering if I should have Spitter come rape your ass? No, you don't have to worry about that, and don't even flatter yourself. He fucking this pussy here."

"So now who ain't loyal? You fucking a nigga who just got out of prison, who was your baby daddy's best friend."

"Yeah, and I guess Boo was your way of getting back at him. See, you ain't loyal, just like the song. I'm not one of those hoes. I know Robb was fucking you, and I still wanted him because he was mine. He could fuck any hoe out on the street because he knew he had a loyal bitch to come home to. I'm loyal to a fault, but I'm not a thot, if you follow me. I didn't like it, and I tried to control the hoe population, but it didn't work. Obviously...because you and your nigga Harvey had the pigs shoot his ass! Now I ain't got nobody. There's a code on the street that when your nigga dies, his boy takes care of you. That's Spitter's job."

"You're fucking crazy."

Yvette, who was wearing Timberland boots at the time, kicked Keysha in the face and stomach hard, causing her to fall over in the chair.

Lifting it back up, Yvette said, "you can kiss my ass, bitch! I'm not fucking crazy. Don't you dare call me crazy. You're a crazy ass hoe who thinks that every nigga needs to bow down and kiss your feet literally. No, not going to happen with Spitter. In fact, bring those little niggas out here!"

On command, Spitter brought out the boys. Both were scared and still.

As Spitter pointed the gun to their heads, Yvette said, "let's play a game. Let's see who lives and who dies. Do you want Harvey's son to get blasted? No skin off your fat ass. He's not yours, and you get off free and clear. Or do you want your bastard son dead? Son of a Chinese delivery driver. That just shows how much of a hoe you really are, but I can understand why you don't want him killed. He's your meal ticket because no matter what color someone is, the color of money is always green."

"Kill me!" Keysha cried. "Kill me!"

"Bitch, you don't get off that easily. No, you do not! You don't get to die until you beg for death, nigga bitch!"

CHAPTER 17

Outside, Detective Weinstein and Harvey met a lot of officers downstairs in front of the building.

"Yvette Carter, this is Detective Weinstein. We do have the place surrounded, please release your hostages and come out. No one gets hurt."

"Hostages?" Harvey asked.

"Yes, I'm sorry I deceived you, but I didn't want you to do anything crazy."

"Who's Yvette Carter?" Harvey asked.

"Yvette Carter is Robb's ex-girlfriend, and they have a child together. She wasn't too happy about Robb getting shot and voiced her opinions very openly. We've had her under surveillance ever since the funeral. We hoped that she would contact Spitter, and she did. What we didn't know was he would kill Stephanie and Boo."

"You mean this idiot was on the loose, and you did nothing about it?" Harvey asked upset.

"There was nothing we could do at the time. He was legitimately out on bail, and we followed him but lost track of him a couple of days after he got out. Then all of a sudden, Boo was murdered then Stephanie was murdered. It was a no brainer who was behind them."

"So what does this have to do with me and Keysha?"

"I knew you two hooked up a lot randomly. It was no secret that you two were at the center of all this, especially on Keysha's side. Right now, Yvette and Spitter are up there with Keysha and..."

A loud gunshot filled the apartment and was heard from outside.

CHAPTER 18

Inside, Keysha's baby was shot on the arm.

"Fool, what in the hell are you doing?!" Yvette shouted.

"My trigger finger got itchy, baby!"

"Nigga what we gon' do now. You shot a fucking kid!"

"I thought that's what we were going to do in the first place."

"No fool, I just wanted to scare this

bitch and let the kids witness their deaths."

"Yeah, but now the police outside. I just got nervous baby. We need to start making plans to get out of here."

"You think?" Yvette said sarcastically.

During their argument, Keysha's head lowered in the greatest of shame. She couldn't believe her child had been shot. She was in a nightmare she hoped would end. She tried to widen her eyes to make sure she wasn't dreaming. Then something strange happened. Though watching her son cry in pain, she watched Harvey's son consoling him. This made Keysha fall in love with Harvey that much more.

"Bitch, this doesn't get you off any

THE HOOK-UP 4: THE FINALE

more than you think it do!" shouted Yvette. "I don't give a fuck who's outside that door. If I have to go out in a blaze of glory, you're going to go out too. I'll bet Harvey's outside right now. I guess he's not as square or soft you told Robb he was. Oh yeah, me and Robb always talked about your shit."

"Fuck you! And I'm glad Robb is dead!" shouted Keysha. "He put his motherfucking hands on me, and I wasn't going to be with weak ass man who put his hands on me!"

Yvette slapped her and yelled back, "don't you ever buck up to me, bitch! You don't know me!"

Keysha started laughing hysterically with her mouth bleeding.

"What the fuck is so funny? You're

the one naked, tied up, and humiliated in front of your child whose now shot and needing medical attention."

"Because you think you're the one with all the power. You may be able to shoot me, kill me, and you may be able to shoot children, but there's no way you're getting out of here alive. So it looks like we'll all be joining your baby daddy real soon."

"Oh you got an answer for everything don't you, bitch? Well, let me tell you something. These little mind games you're playing aren't helping."

CHAPTER 19

Outside, Harvey said a little prayer and then really thought back to his first encounter with Keysha. He wondered if he had been a man and handled his business with Susan in the first place how things would have turned out. Last time he checked, Susan was married and doing well. Harvey hoped to be married by now and in a better place this.

Right now, everyone he loved was upstairs. All three of them. He needed to get upstairs in order to save them, but he knew Weinstein wouldn't let him.

"Detective," Harvey pleaded. "I need to get upstairs to do something."

"Leave this to the professionals, son. They'll be fine, I promise."

Upset, Harvey replied, "you promise? There's been a gunshot in the apartment. Not out the window, not at you guys, in the apartment."

"Calm down and be patient."

"You've been on that little loudspeaker for almost an hour and no one's answered. My loved ones could be dead by now, and no one even knows if they're okay."

"So what do you expect me to do? Last time I checked, you're a civilian, and you definitely don't have an 'S' on your chest. So you need to take a step back and..."

Harvey broke away from the police units and ran through the back way, into his apartment. Quietly, using his key, he thought he was being careful coming in until....

"You were stupid for coming here, mane," said Spitter, who greeted Harvey with a gun to his head. "I oughtta blast you in the fucking head right now, but I'll bet you want to see your family."

Harvey walked into the living room to find a naked, teary eyed Keysha and her baby who'd been shot with his son consoling him.

"What's up?" Harvey asked. "Why did you have to shoot the kids?

Whatever beef you had is with me and Keysha. Why the babies?"

Yvette answered, "first, nigga, shut the fuck up! You speak when you're spoken to. Number two, do you think I wanted to shoot the kid? That was my trigger happy boyfriend, and he wouldn't have been so trigger happy if your woman wasn't talking shit."

Harvey pleaded, "look, you've proved your point, but please let Keysha and the babies go. I'll stay and..."

Yvette replied, "look at this nigga here! You suddenly have some balls. You didn't have any when you cheated on your woman with this hoe in the first place, without protection. Then you let this thot lie to you on every count. She don't love you, and she wouldn't do the same if the shoe was on the other foot. Nigga, you's a fool."

"It doesn't matter if she loves me or not. I love her, and I care for her son. I love that boy just as much as I love mine. And right now, I just care for their safety."

"Spitter, check this fool for a wire."

He searched Harvey but didn't find any.

"Oh, so you're some big hero now, huh?" said Yvette. "You want to defend a bitch who played you with my nigga! A bitch who tried to pin a baby on you that wasn't even yours. Nigga you a bigger fool than I thought. I really was just going to fuck with you by cancelling this bitch then leave you alone, but I see your little noble man act is going to get you killed. See, there are no real nice guys in the world because either you're trying to be fake, or they get killed for being themselves."

"Spitter, get over here!" Yvette commanded.

He walked over to Keysha and gave her a soft kiss on the cheek before putting a gun to her head and cocking it.

"Say goodbye to your bitch!"

"Police freeze!" Just then Detective Weinstein and about five officers bust in through the back just as Harvey had.

Spitter grabbed Keysha closer and said, "No, you freeze, you pig bitches, or I'll splatter this bitch's brains..."

His speech was interrupted by Harvey who tackled Spitter. Spitter held the gun tight in his grip during the fight with Harvey. During the struggle, the gun went off, and everything went black...

CHAPTER 20

Three Years Later....

Keysha and Harvey were finally free. The couple moved to Virginia Beach where their days and nights were filled with more passion than ever before. To think, their life had started with one hook up. Oh, before we conclude the story, a quick update.

The moment the gun went off, Harvey was hit in the arm and police tackled both Spitter and Yvette. Both were sent to prison for fifty years each for aggravated assault, false imprisonment, murder and accessory to murder, in addition to a list of other charges. Both Harvey and Keysha's son survived their injuries.

Now the demons that haunted them both have both been calmed. No more hook ups.

The End

ABOUT THE PUBLISHER

Jerrice Owens Presents, also known as JOP, is dedicated to providing high quality stories in a variety of genres. While our primary focus is urban lit, we are graciously expanding into new territories. Currently we have works in African American Christian lit, urban erotica, street lit, contemporary urban fiction, and hood romance.